P9-CBL-800

A VISIT TO
France

REVISED AND UPDATED

NORTH
AMERICA

FRANCE EUROPE

ASIA

AFRICA

SOUTH
AMERICA

AUSTRALIA

Rob Alcraft

Heinemann Library
Chicago, Illinois

©2008 Heinemann Library
a division of Pearson, Ltd.
Chicago, Illinois

Customer Service 888-454-2279

Visit our website at www.heinemannlibrary.com

Designed by Heinemann Library
Printed in the United States, North Mankato, MN

12 11 10
10 9 8 7 6 5 4 3 2

Library of Congress Cataloging-in-Publication Data
Alcraft, Rob, 1966-.
    France / by Rob Alcraft.
        p. cm. – (A visit to)
    Included bibliographical references and index.
    Summary: Introduces the land, landmarks, homes, food, clothing, work,
    transportation, language, and culture of Egypt.
    ISBN: 978-1-4329-1266-6 (lib.bdg.); 978-1-4329-1285-7 (pbk)
        1. France—Pictorial works—Juvenile literature. I. Title. II. Title: France. III. Series.
DT20.A55
944—dc21
                                            99-19129

Acknowledgements
The publishers would like to thank the following for permission to reproduce photographs: ©Bridgeman Art Library p. **28**; ©Getty Images p. **11** (The Image Bank/Michael Melford), p. **24** (The Image Bank/Yellow Dog Productions); ©J Allan Cash pp. **17**, **25**; ©Masterfile p. **13** (Bruce Fleming); ©Photolibrary p. **18** (Mauritius/ Raga Raga), p. **19** (Photononstop/A J Cassaigne); ©Rex Features p. **29** (Sipa Press); ©Robert Harding Picture Library p. **9**, p. **5** (Robert Francis), p. **6** (Adam Woolfitt), p. **15** (Nik Wheeler), p. **21** (K Gillham), p. **26** (Tomlinson); ©Telegraph Colour Library p. **16** (C B Knight), p. **27** (Kathy Collins); ©Trevor Clifford p. **17**; ©Trip p. **7** (D Hastilow), p. **8** (A Tovy), p. **10** (J Braund), p. **12** (A M Bazalik), p. **22** (Ask Images), p. **20** (S Grant), p. **23** (R Cracknell).

Cover photograph of the Pyramide and Palais du Louvre, Musee du Lourve, Paris, France reproduced with permission of Robert Harding (Nigel Francis).

Our thanks to Nick Lapthorn and Clare Lewis for their help in the preparation of this book.

062010
Booksource

Contents

Any words appearing in bold, **like this**, are explained in the Glossary.

France

Key
- Land above 3,200ft
- Land above 1,600ft
- Land above 650ft
- Land above 0ft/sea level
- ● Capital
- Å Eiffel Tower
- �X Pont du Gard
- –·– Boundary

ENGLAND

ENGLISH CHANNEL

BELGIUM

GERMANY

R. Somme

Paris

R. Seine

R. Loire

North

F R A N C E

SWITZERLAND

R. Dordogne

R. Rhône

A L P S

ITALY

Cannes

Pyrénées

SPAIN

MEDITERRANEAN SEA

France is a big country. It is in Europe.

A quarter of France is forest. There are lakes and rivers. There are gentle valleys where grapes grow. A place where grapes are grown is called a vineyard.

France is famous for its vineyards.

DOMAINE R COULY

Land

In the north of France there are green fields and **meadows**. The weather is cool, and it often rains. Farmers grow **wheat** and keep cows.

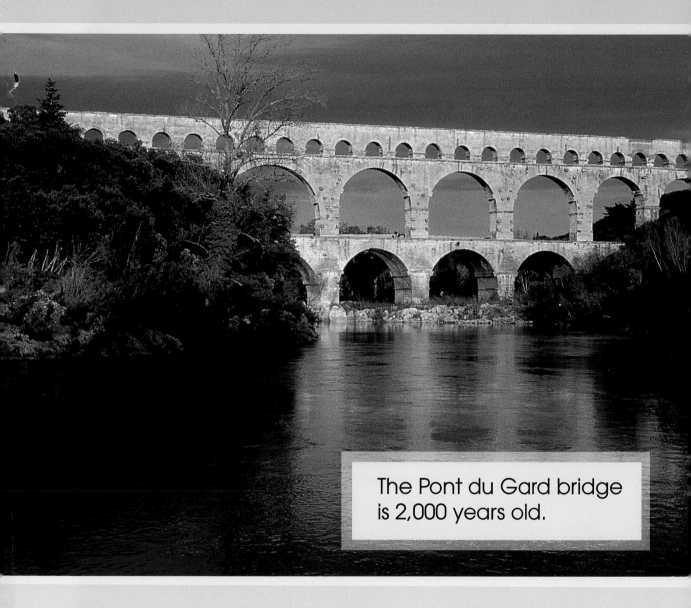

The Pont du Gard bridge is 2,000 years old.

This is a bridge, called the Pont du Gard. It was built to carry water to an ancient city.

Homes

In cities like Paris most people live in apartments. Some windows have wooden **shutters** to keep the rooms cool in summer.

Many smaller towns and villages in France are very old. There are shady squares and narrow streets. The old houses are built from stone.

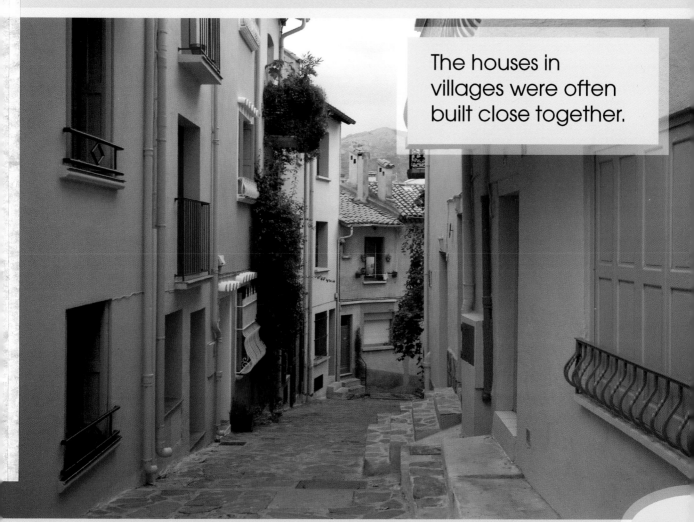

The houses in villages were often built close together.

Food

Each **region** of France makes its own kinds of cheese, sausage and wine. A good snack is local cheese, with a long stick of French bread.

In France, people often have meals outside.

In France, families often sit together to eat. This family is enjoying lunch outside in the garden.

Clothes

Many French people wear jeans, tennis shoes and colorful T-shirts, or sweaters and coats. Some people wear a special French hat called a béret.

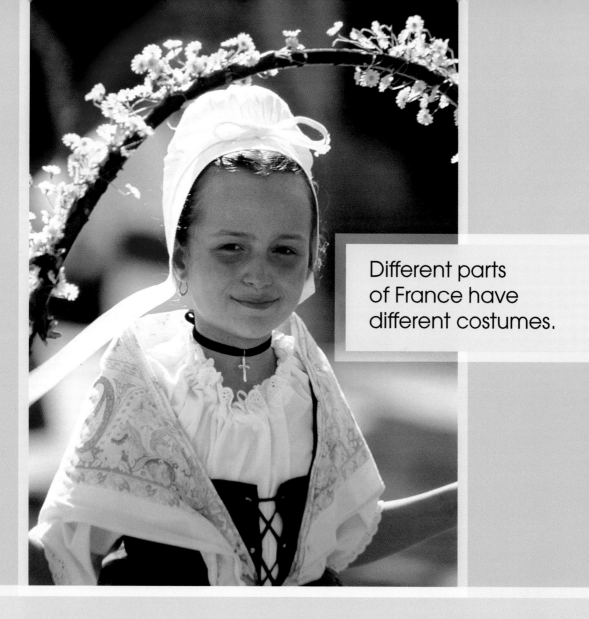

Different parts
of France have
different costumes.

For festivals and parties people still dress up in old French costumes. Women wear white blouses, **bonnets**, and long black skirts with colorful patterns.

Work

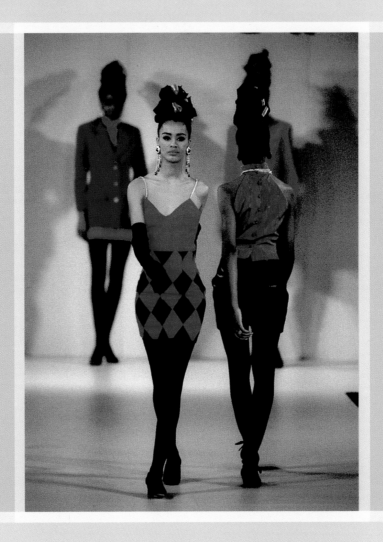

France is famous for its **fashion**.
Some people have jobs in the fashion
industry, making and selling clothes.

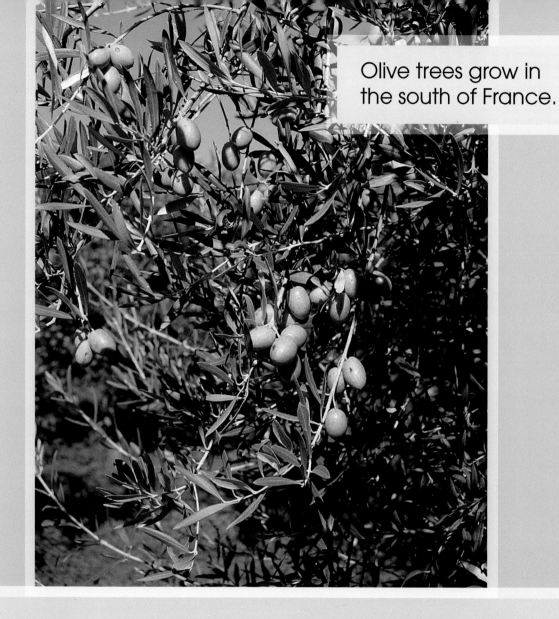

Olive trees grow in the south of France.

In the country, many farmers grow olive trees. The olives can be eaten or made into oil for cooking.

Transportation

France has very fast highways. You have to pay to use them. One of the busiest highways runs around Paris. This one runs over a huge bridge.

This is called a TGV train. It can go over 300 miles per hour.

French trains are comfortable and very fast. The **canals** and rivers are busy with **barges** and boats. There are airports in most cities, too.

Languages

In France people speak French. French sounds very different from English, but it uses the same alphabet.

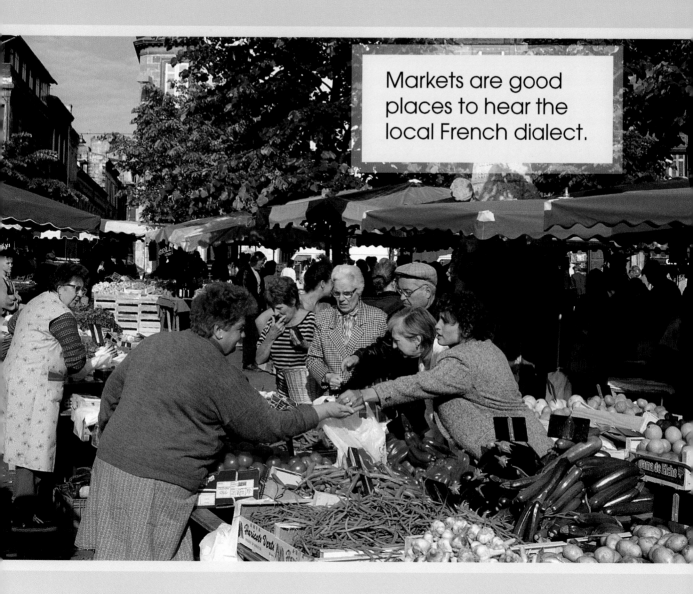

Markets are good places to hear the local French dialect.

Different **regions** of France have their own **dialects**. French is also spoken in many other parts of the world.

School

Most French children go to school six days a week. Wednesday afternoons are free. French children study many subjects, including math, geography, and English.

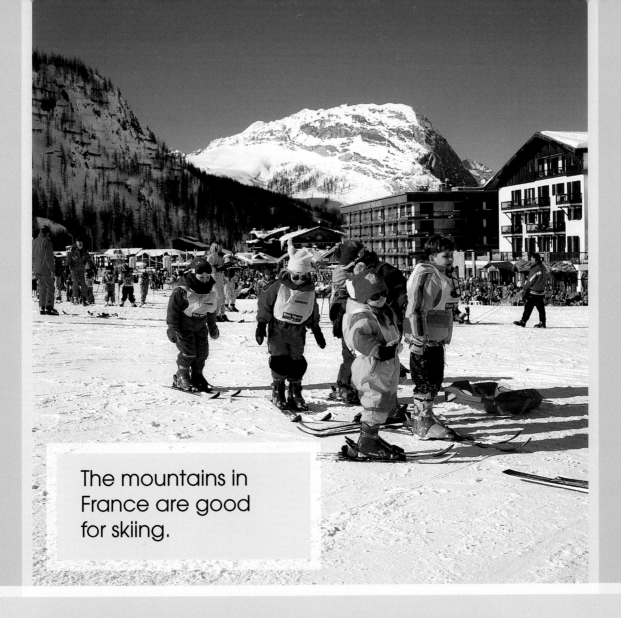

The mountains in France are good for skiing.

Some French schools have special holidays. The whole class will go off for a week for lessons by the beach. In the winter the class might go off to learn how to ski.

Free Time

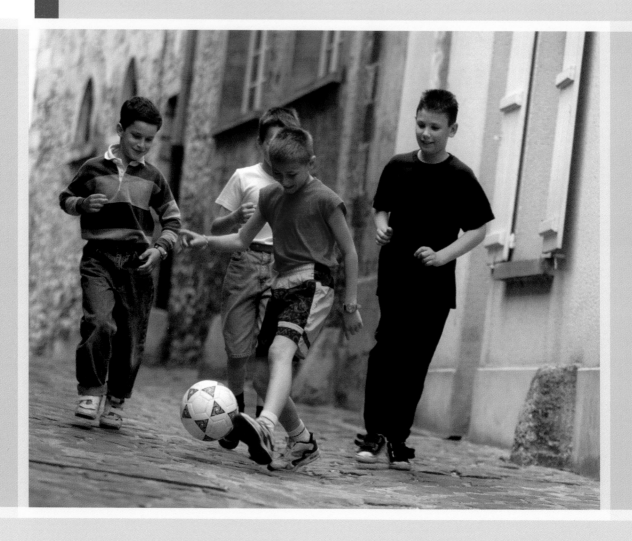

Young people play sports like soccer in parks or in the street. Sometimes they watch TV or visit friends. In the summer they might go swimming at the beach.

On warm summer evenings many French people like to sit in pavement cafés and watch the world go by. Some people play a game called **pétanque**.

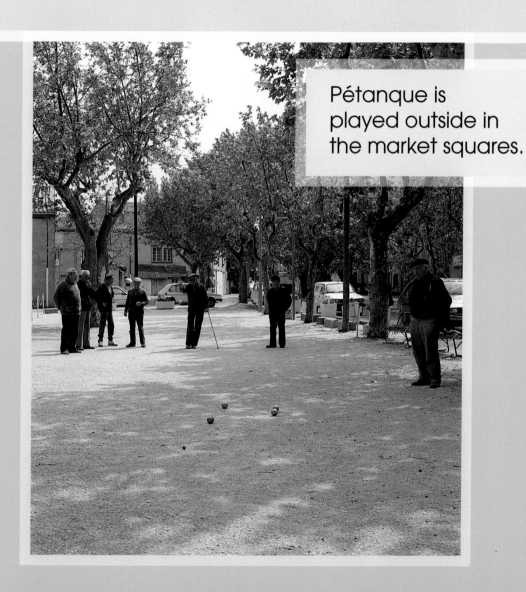

Pétanque is played outside in the market squares.

Celebrations

One of the biggest celebrations in France is called Mardi Gras. Everyone has a big party, and there are fireworks and **parades** along city streets.

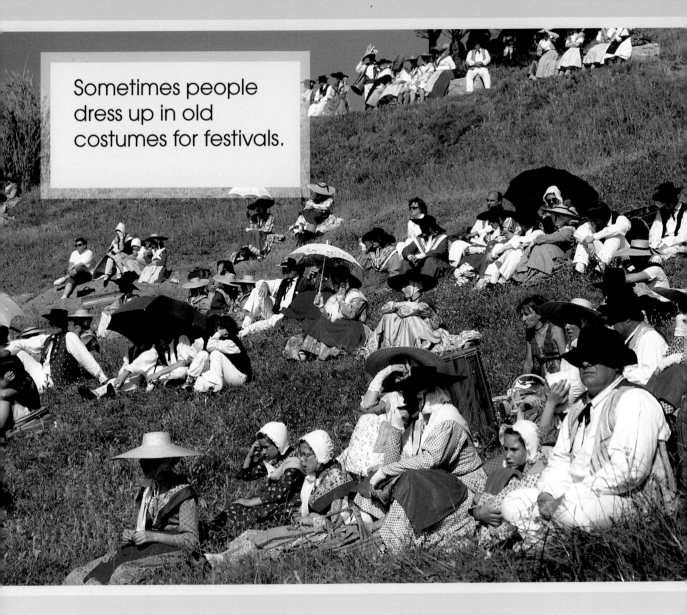

Sometimes people dress up in old costumes for festivals.

Many French towns and villages have their own special celebration or festival. It might be on a Saint's Day, or to celebrate the **harvest**. Some are in honor of the local cheese, or that year's new wine.

The Arts

There have been many famous French painters. This is a painting by Renoir. He wanted his paintings to show how beautiful and colorful the world is.

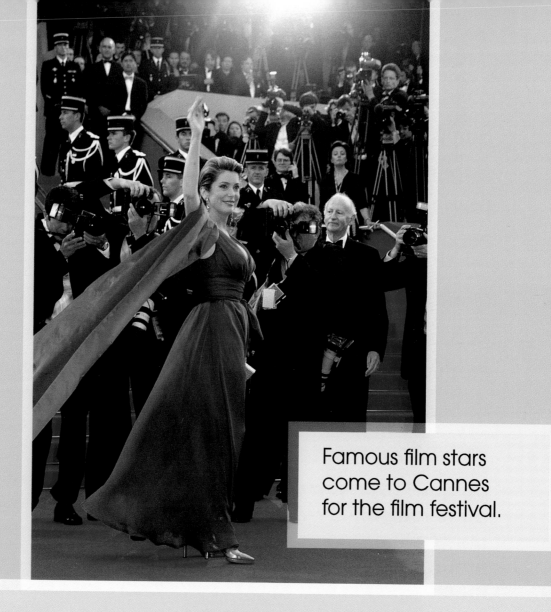

Famous film stars come to Cannes for the film festival.

Making films is important in France. In May there is a special film festival at a town called Cannes. People come from all over the world to see the new films.

Factfile

Name	The French Republic
Capital	France's **capital** city is called Paris.
Language	French
Population	There are 64 million people living in France.
Money	French money is called the euro.
Religions	Most French people are Christians.
Products	France makes cars, cloth, aircraft, machines and **electrical goods**. **Tourism** is also very important.

Words You CanLearn

bonjour (bon-jewer)	hello
au revoir (oh-rev-wa)	goodbye
oui (we)	yes
non (noh)	no
merci (ma-r-see)	thank you
S'il vous plaît (cil voo play)	please
un (urn)	one
deux (de)	two
trois (twa)	three

Glossary

barge a boat with a flat bottom. It can float in shallow water.

bonnet a kind of hat that women wear

canal a river dug by people

capital the city where the government is based

dialect the language spoken by people in one area

electrical goods things like televisions and videos which use electricity

fashion the way clothes look and what color they are

harvest the time when fruit, vegetables and other crops are ready for the farmer to pick

meadow grassy land

parade special carnival in the street

pétanque a game like bowls

region a part of a country

shutters wooden flaps on each side of a window. They can be closed to keep the light out.

tourism everything to do with visiting a place on holiday

wheat plant used to make flour

Index